STORIES FOR BEDTIME

Compiled by Fiona Waters

Illustrated by Penny Dann

ORCHARD BOOKS

for Victoria and Hannah,
with much love
F.W.

for Jackie
P.D.

This selection copyright © Fiona Waters 1991
Illustrations copyright © Penny Dann 1991
First published in Great Britain in 1991 by
ORCHARD BOOKS
96 Leonard Street, London, EC2A 4RH
Orchard Books Australia
14 Mars Road, Lane Cove, NSW 2066
1 85213 243 4
Printed in Hong Kong
Reprinted 1991, 1992

A CIP catalogue record for this book is available from the British Library.

Contents

The Flying Rabbit KENNETH McLEISH 5

Cheese, Peas and Chocolate Pudding BETTY VAN WITSEN 12

The Beast with a Thousand Teeth TERRY JONES 17

Victoria and the Crowded Pocket CAROLYN SLOAN 25

The Little Witch MARGARET MAHY 29

Junk Day on Juniper Street LILIAN MOORE 34

The Animals' Garden ANITA HEWETT 41

Big Sister and Little Sister CHARLOTTE ZOLOTOW 48

The Giant Who Threw Tantrums DAVID L. HARRISON 52

The Little Girl's Medicine MARGARET WISE BROWN 59

Big Bakes a Cake SUE LIMB 67

The Fat Princess WENDY EYTON 73

The Flying Rabbit

KENNETH McLEISH

One day, Small Rabbit was out in the meadow, as usual. He looked up at the birds in the sky. He thought to himself, "I'm tired of walking about on the ground all the time. I'm going to fly, like the birds."

He climbed a tree. It wasn't easy, because his front legs were too short and his back legs were too long.

When he was half way up, he looked down. The ground was a long way off. "All right," he thought. "Now's the time to fly!"

He spread his front legs out like wings, and gave a great big rabbit-jump off his branch.

But he was lucky, for just underneath his flying-branch was the nest of the Crow family. He landed in it with a bump.

"Ow!" said the two little crows. "Watch where you're falling!"

Small Rabbit didn't answer. He was wondering why he hadn't been able to fly. "Can you fly?" he asked the little crows.

"Not yet," they answered. "But we will one day, if we try hard enough."

"So will I," said Small Rabbit. "I'll stay here with you until then."

Small Rabbit stayed in the Crows' nest all day. It was a bit of a squeeze, especially when Mr and Mrs Crow came back. They weren't pleased to find a new rabbit baby in their nest.

As it began to get dark, Mrs Rabbit noticed that Small was missing. She went out to the edge of the field to look for him. "Small?" she called. "Sma-all! Where are you?"

"Up here," said Small, poking his head over the side of the Crows' nest.

"Good gracious! Whatever are you doing up there?" asked Mrs Rabbit.

"Learning to fly."

"Come down, you silly child. Rabbits don't fly."

"I won't come down."

His mother went back to the burrow and fetched Mr Rabbit. He came and sat beside her under the tree. "Be careful, Small," he said. "It's a long way down."

All the nine little rabbits came too. They all sat in a row under the tree, looking up at Small.

No one knew what to do. Mr and Mrs Crow began to get cross. "Look," they said to Small. "You can't stay here all night. There isn't room."

"It won't take all night," answered Small. "As soon as I can fly, I'll go."

"But rabbits can't fly," shouted the Crows.

"In that case, I'll make history," said Small.

The Crows got angrier and angrier. The two baby crows were squashed under Small's furry tail. The big crows had to sit hanging over the edge of the nest. They looked like umbrellas that hadn't been folded up properly.

At last Mr Crow lost his temper. "You stay here," he said to Mrs Crow. "I'm going out." And off he flew.

So there they all sat, eleven rabbits in the field under the tree, and one rabbit and three crows in the nest. The biggest crow was hanging over the edge. The shadows of night began to creep across the field.

Mr Crow was away a long time. At last, as the sun was beginning to disappear behind the hills, he came flying back. He landed on the side of the nest, and nearly fell off again, there was so little room.

"It's all right," he said. "I've been to see Owl and he's told me what to do."

"What did he say?" asked Mrs Crow.

"Come up here and I'll tell you," said Mr Crow.

Mr and Mrs Crow flew to a branch higher up the tree, and he whispered into her ear behind his wing. No one else said anything. The eleven rabbits in the field, and the one rabbit and two crows in the nest, sat still and waited.

At last Mr and Mrs Crow came back. "Come on, little crows," said Mr Crow. "Time to be going."

"Going? Going where?" said the little crows.

"To the rabbit warren, of course. If rabbits are going to start flying, crows will have to start living in holes in the ground. Down we go!"

He picked up one of the little crows in his beak, and flew off. Mrs Crow elbowed Small out of the way with her wing, and flew off with the other little crow. They circled round and down, towards the rabbit burrow on the other side of the field.

Small watched them go. All at once he began to feel lonely. The sun had almost gone. He was getting cold, all on his own in the nest. He looked down. The eleven rabbits from his family were still sitting on the ground watching him.

"I . . . I think I'd better come down," he said.

"All right," said Mr Rabbit. "Are you going to fly?"

"Not today. I don't feel much like flying any more. Rabbits ought to stay on the ground, and leave flying to the birds."

"How will you get down then?"

"I'll have to jump," said Small nervously. "Will you catch me?"

"You can't jump," his mother said. "You'll hurt yourself."

"I know!" said Mr Rabbit suddenly. He whispered to the other rabbits. Then he and Mrs Rabbit lay down, and Large climbed on to their backs. When he was ready the Medium Twins climbed up and balanced on top of his head. Then the bravest of the Triplets climbed up and stood on their heads. Soon there was a ladder of rabbits, reaching all the way up to the Crows' nest. The baby rabbits were too small to climb, but they stood by ready to catch anyone who fell.

"Come on, Small," said Mr Rabbit in a squashed sort of voice. "Be quick, before we all fall over."

As soon as Small was down, the rabbit ladder unsorted itself.

"Thank goodness for that," said Mr Rabbit. "It was flat work being at the bottom."

"Don't ever do a thing like that again," said Mrs Rabbit crossly to Small. "Look what's happened now. We've got a family of Crows moved into our burrow. How are we going to get rid of them?"

But there was no need. As soon as the Crow family saw that their nest was empty, they flew back and put the baby crows safely inside it. "We'll move into a new one tomorrow. As high as we can go," said Mr Crow.

That's why, if you go and look, you'll find that all crows live in nests right at the top of very high trees. And rabbits stay on the ground.

Cheese, Peas and Chocolate Pudding

BETTY VAN WITSEN

There was once a little boy who ate cheese, peas and chocolate pudding. Cheese, peas and chocolate pudding. Cheese, peas and chocolate pudding. Every day the same old things: cheese, peas and chocolate pudding.

For breakfast he would have some cheese. Any kind. Cream cheese, American cheese, Swiss cheese, Dutch cheese, Italian cheese, blue cheese, green cheese, yellow cheese, brick cheese. Just cheese for breakfast.

For lunch he ate peas. Green or yellow peas. Frozen peas, canned peas, dried peas, split peas, black-eyed peas. No potatoes — just peas for lunch.

And for supper he would have cheese and peas. And chocolate pudding. Cheese, peas and chocolate pudding.

Cheese, peas and chocolate pudding. Every day the same old things: cheese, peas and chocolate pudding.

Once his mother bought a lamb chop for him. She cooked it in a little frying pan on the stove and she put some salt on it, and gave it to the little boy on a little blue dish. The boy looked at it. He smelled it. (It did smell delicious!) He even touched it. But . . .

"Is this cheese?" he asked.

"It's a lamb chop, darling," said his mother.

The boy shook his head. "Cheese!" he said. So his mother ate the lamb chop herself, and the boy had some cottage cheese.

One day his big brother was chewing a raw carrot. It sounded so good, the little boy reached his hand out for a bite.

"Sure!" said his brother. "Here!" The little boy almost put the carrot in his mouth, but at the last minute he remembered, and he said, "Is this peas?"

"No, it's a carrot," said his brother.

"Peas," said the little boy firmly, handing the carrot back.

Once his daddy was eating a big dish of raspberry jelly. It looked so shiny red and cool, the little boy came over and held his mouth open.

"Want a taste?" asked his daddy. The little boy looked and looked at the jelly. He almost looked it off the dish. But: "Is it chocolate pudding?" he asked.

"No, son, it's jelly," said his daddy.

So the little boy frowned and backed away. "Chocolate pudding!" he said.

His grandma baked cookies for him. His grandpa bought him an ice cream cone. The little boy just shook his head.

His aunt and uncle invited him for a fried chicken dinner. Everybody ate fried chicken and more fried chicken. Except the little boy. And you know what he ate.

Cheese, peas and chocolate pudding. Cheese, peas and chocolate pudding. Every day the same old things: cheese, peas and chocolate pudding.

But one day — ah, one day, a very funny thing happened. The little boy was playing puppy. He lay on the floor and growled and barked and rolled over. He crept to the table where his big brother was having lunch.

"Arf-arf!" he barked.

"Good doggie!" said his brother, patting his head. The little boy lay down on his back on the floor and barked again.

But at that minute, his big brother dropped a piece of *something* from his plate. And the little boy's mouth was just ready to say "Arf!". And what do you think happened?

Something dropped into the little boy's mouth. He sat up in surprise. Because *something* was on his tongue. And *something* was warm and juicy and delicious!

And it didn't taste like cheese. And it didn't taste like peas. And it certainly wasn't chocolate pudding.

The little boy chewed slowly. Each chew tasted better than the last. He swallowed *something* and opened his mouth again. Wide. As wide as he could.

"Want some more?" asked his brother.

The little boy closed his mouth and thought.

"That's not cheese," he said.

"No, it's not," said his brother.

"And it isn't peas."

"No, not peas," said his brother.

"And it couldn't be chocolate pudding."

"No, it certainly is not chocolate pudding," smiled his brother. "It's hamburger."

The little boy thought hard.

"I like hamburger," he said.

So his big brother shared the rest of his hamburger with him, and ever after that, guess what! Ever after that, the little boy ate cheese, peas and chocolate pudding and hamburger.

Until he was your age, of course. When he was your age, he ate everything.

The Beast with a Thousand Teeth

TERRY JONES

A long time ago, in a land far away, the most terrible beast that ever lived roamed the countryside. It had four eyes, six legs and a thousand teeth. In the morning it would gobble up men as they went to work in the fields. In the afternoon it would break into lonely farms and eat up mothers and children as they sat down to lunch, and at night it would stalk the streets of the towns, looking for its supper.

In the biggest of all the towns, there lived a pastrycook and his wife, and they had a small son whose name was Sam. One morning, as Sam was helping his father to make pastries, he heard that the Mayor had offered a reward of ten bags of gold to anyone who could rid the city of the beast.

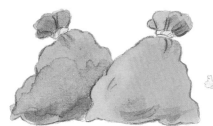

"Oh," said Sam, "wouldn't I just like to win those ten bags of gold!"

"Nonsense!" said his father. "Put those pastries in the oven."

That afternoon, they heard that the King himself had offered a reward of a hundred bags of gold to anyone who could rid the kingdom of the beast.

"Oooh! Wouldn't I just like to win those hundred bags of gold," said Sam.

"You're too small," said his father. "Now run along and take those cakes to the Palace before it gets dark."

So Sam set off for the Palace with a tray of cakes balanced on his head. But he was so busy thinking of the hundred bags of gold that he lost his way, and it began to grow dark.

"Oh dear!" said Sam. "The beast will be coming soon to look for his supper. I'd better hurry home."

So he turned and started to hurry home as fast as he could. But he was utterly and completely lost, and he didn't know which way to turn. Soon it grew very dark. The streets were deserted, and everyone was safe inside, and had bolted their doors for fear of the beast.

Poor Sam ran up this street and down the next, but he couldn't find the way home. Then suddenly — in the distance — he heard a sound like thunder, and he knew that the beast with a thousand teeth was approaching the city!

Sam ran up to the nearest house, and started to bang on the door.

"Let me in!" he cried. "I'm out in the streets, and the beast is approaching the city! Listen!" And he could hear the sound of the beast getting nearer and nearer. The ground shook and the windows rattled in their frames. But the people inside said no — if they opened the door, the beast might get in and eat them too.

So poor Sam ran up to the next house, and banged as hard as he could on their door, but the people told him to go away.

Then he heard a roar, and he heard the beast coming down the street, and he ran as hard as he could. But no matter how hard he ran, he could hear the beast getting nearer . . . and nearer . . . And he glanced over his shoulder — and there it was at the end of the street! Poor Sam in his fright dropped his tray, and hid under some steps. And the beast got nearer and nearer until it was right on top of him, and it bent down and its terrible jaws went SNACK! and it gobbled up the tray of cakes, and then it turned on Sam.

Sam plucked up all his courage as he shouted as loud as he could: "Don't eat me, Beast! Wouldn't you rather have some more cakes?"

The beast stopped and looked at Sam, and then it looked back at the empty tray, and it said: "Well . . . they were very nice cakes . . ." And it reached under the steps where poor Sam was hiding, and pulled him out in its great horny claws.

"Oh . . . p-p-please!" cried Sam. "If you don't eat me, I'll make you some more. I'll make you lots of good things, for I'm the son of the best pastrycook in the land."

"Will you make more of those pink ones?" asked the beast.

"Oh yes! I'll make you as many pink ones as you can eat!" cried Sam.

"Very well," said the beast, and put poor Sam in his pocket, and carried him home to his lair.

The beast lived in a dark and dismal cave. The floor was littered with the bones of the people it had eaten, and the stone walls were marked with lines, where the beast used to sharpen its teeth. But Sam got to work right away, and started to bake as many cakes as he could for the beast. And when he ran out of flour or eggs or anything else, the beast would run back into town to get them, although it never paid for anything.

Sam cooked and baked, and he made scones and éclairs and meringues and sponge cakes and shortbread and doughnuts. But the beast looked at them and said, "You haven't made any pink ones!"

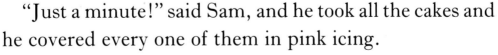

"Just a minute!" said Sam, and he took all the cakes and he covered every one of them in pink icing.

"There you are," said Sam, "they're all pink."

"Great!" said the beast and ate the lot.

Well, the beast grew so fond of Sam's cakes that it shortly gave up eating people altogether, and it stayed at home in its cave eating and eating, and growing fatter and fatter. This went on for a whole year, until one morning Sam woke up to find the beast rolling around groaning and beating the floor. Of course you can guess what was the matter with it.

"Oh dear," said Sam, "I'm afraid it's all that pink icing that has given you toothache."

Well, the toothache got worse and worse and, because the beast had a thousand teeth, it was soon suffering from the worst toothache that anyone in the whole history of the world has ever suffered from. It lay on its side and held its head and roared in agony, until Sam began to feel quite sorry for it. The beast howled and howled with pain, until it could stand it no longer. "Please, Sam, help me!" it cried.

"Very well," said Sam. "Sit still and open your mouth."
So the beast sat very still and opened its mouth, while Sam got a pair of pliers and took out every single tooth in the beast's head.

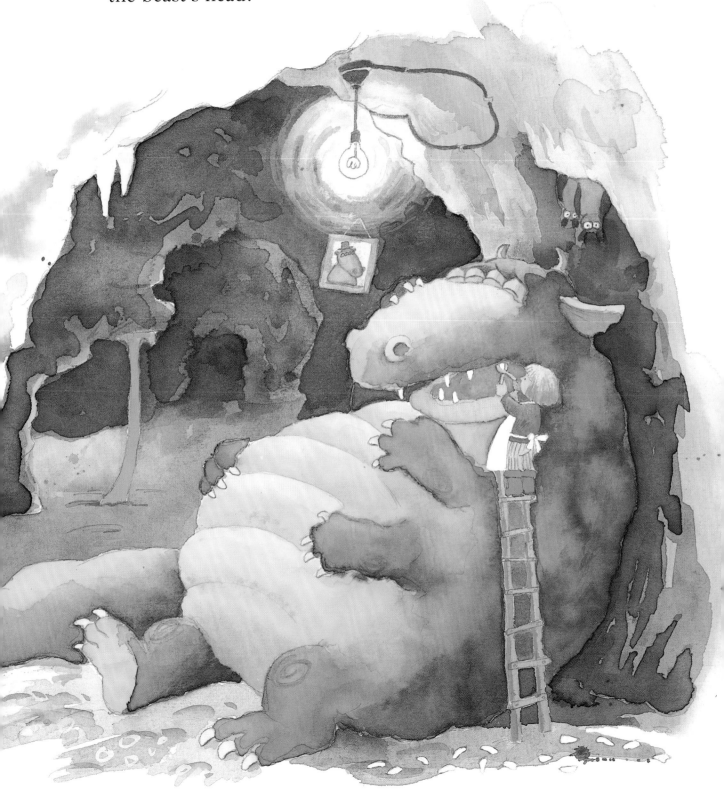

Well, when the beast had lost all its thousand teeth, it couldn't eat people any more. So Sam took it home and went to the Mayor and claimed ten bags of gold as his reward. Then he went to the King and claimed the hundred bags of gold as his reward. Then he went back and lived with his father and mother once more, and the beast helped in the pastryshop, and took cakes to the Palace every day, and everyone forgot they had ever been afraid of the beast with a thousand teeth.

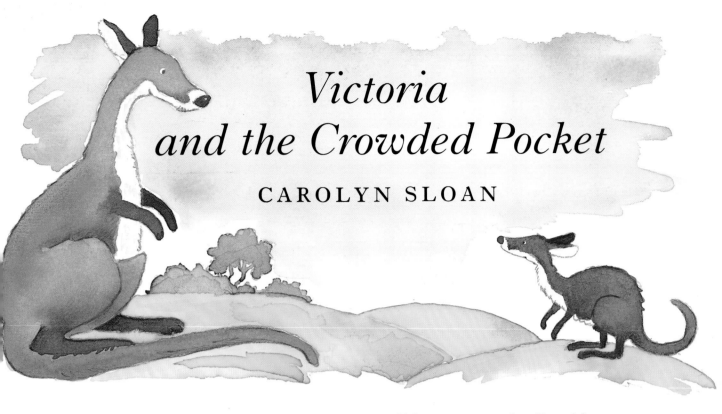

Victoria
and the Crowded Pocket

CAROLYN SLOAN

When Victoria was a very small kangaroo, she lived in her mother's pocket. It was not a staying-still place, like a house. It was like living in a flying jumble sale. There were keys and coathangers in the pocket, and tins of treacle and candles and sometimes cheese sandwiches.

One day, when her mother had bounced about very badly, Victoria jumped out of the pocket.

"I have had enough," she said. "I'm sticky and bruised. That pocket is a MESS."

Victoria went to Mrs Koala.

"Please let me live the way your children live," she said. "It is terrible in my mother's pocket."

"All right," said the Koala Bear kindly. "Climb on my back and STAY on."

Away they went through the trees. Victoria fell off into a puddle and was scratched by a tree.

"Thank you, Mrs Koala," she gasped when they stopped. "But it's safer in my mother's pocket; I will go back there."

Victoria hopped back to her mother, and for a while she was very happy. Then her mother found a spiky cactus in a pot and a goldfish in a bowl, and put them in her pocket on top of Victoria.

The water slopped out of the bowl, and the cactus poked Victoria with its sharp spikes.

"I can't live in this muddy, spiky mess," she said, and jumped out.

She went to Mrs Rabbit and said: "Please take me home with you. I want to live the way your children live."

"Please yourself," said the rabbit, and she started to run very fast.

The little kangaroo was running out of bounce when Mrs Rabbit suddenly shot down a hole.

"You can't live down a hole," puffed Victoria.

But Mrs Rabbit did. The hole was just big enough for her but much too small for Victoria.

"This is no place to live," said Victoria. "It's too small for me. Thank you, Mrs Rabbit, but I will go back to my mother's pocket."

Mrs Kangaroo spring-cleaned her pocket, and for a little while it was a good place to be. But soon she began to find all sorts of things which she put in the pocket on top of Victoria.

She found a wrist watch, a feather, a fountain pen, a mushroom, a cup and a saucer, some nuts and bolts, a book, a box of matches, some cotton reels, a spoon and a fork, a squashed tube of paint, and a cricket bat.

Victoria had to move out again. She went to the lake and found Mrs Goose. "Please let me live the way your children live," she said.

And so she joined the little geese in their wet and spiky nest.

"You will have to hang your long feet over the edge," said Mrs Goose.

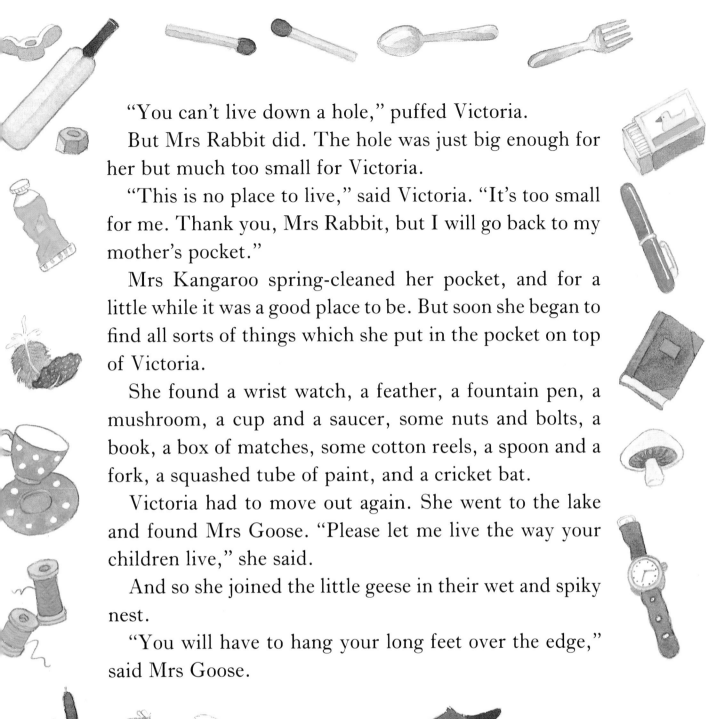

After two wet and spiky days, Victoria got out of the nest.

"I'm sorry," she said to the geese, "but it isn't a kangaroo sort of nest."

Victoria wandered on. Sometimes she stayed a little time with someone, and sometimes she didn't.

In the end she went back to her mother.

"Victoria!" said her mother happily. "Where have you been? How I've missed you!"

Victoria told her mother about the places she had tried to live in that would be better than the pocket.

"But you are too big for my pocket now," said her mother. "There is someone else there now. Look!"

Victoria looked, and there was a baby kangaroo so small that it was hardly there at all. "That is your brother," said Mrs Kangaroo.

"But where shall I live now?" said Victoria.

"With me," said her mother. "We can all three go anywhere we like, and if we don't like it when we get there we can bounce somewhere else."

And the three kangaroos bounced off.

The Little Witch

MARGARET MAHY

The big city was dark. Even the streetlights were out. All day people had gone up and down, up and down; cars and buses had roared and rattled busily along. But now they had all gone home to bed, and only the wind, the shadows, and a small kitten wandered in the wide, still streets.

The kitten chased a piece of paper, pretending it was a mouse. He patted at it with his paws and it flipped behind a rubbish bin. Quick as a wink he leaped after it, and then forgot it because he found something else.

"What is this," he asked the wind, "here asleep behind the rubbish bin? I have never seen it before."

The wind was bowling a newspaper along, but he dropped it and came to see. The great stalking shadows looked down from everywhere.

"Ah," said the wind, "it is a witch ... see her broomstick ... but she is only a very small one."

29

The wind was right. It was a very small witch — a baby one.

The witch heard the wind in her sleep and opened her eyes. Suddenly she was awake.

Far above, the birds peered down at the street below.

"Look!" said the shadows to the sparrows under the eaves. "Look at the little witch; she is such a little witch to be all alone."

"Let me see!" a baby sparrow peeped sleepily.

"Go to sleep!" said his mother. "I didn't hatch you out of the egg to peer at witches all night long."

She snuggled him back into her warm feathers.

But there was no one to snuggle a little witch, wandering cold in the big empty streets, dragging a broom several sizes too big for her. The kitten sprang at the broom. Then he noticed something.

"Wind!" he cried. "See! — wherever this witch walks, she leaves a trail of flowers!"

Yes, it is true! The little witch had lots of magic in her, but she had not learned to use it properly, or to hide it, any more than she had learned to talk.

So wherever she put her feet mignonette grew, and rosemary, violets, lily of the valley, and tiny pink-and-white roses ... all through the streets, and all across the road ...

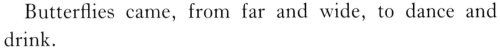

Butterflies came, from far and wide, to dance and drink.

"Who is that down there?" asked a young moth.

"It is a baby witch who has made these fine, crimson feast-rooms for us," a tattered old moth answered.

The wind followed along, playing and juggling with the flowers and their sweet smells. "I shall sweep these all over the city," he said. In their sleep, people smelled the flowers and smiled, dreaming happily.

Now the witch looked up at the tall buildings; windows looked down at her with scorn, and their square sharp shapes seemed angry to her. She pointed her finger at them. Out of the cracks and chinks suddenly crept long twining vines and green leaves. Slowly flowers opened on them ... great crimson flowers like roses, smelling of honey.

The little witch laughed, but in a moment she became solemn. She was so alone. Then the kitten scuttled and pounced at her bare, pink heels, and the little witch knew she had a friend. Dragging her broom for the kitten to chase, she wandered on, leaving a trail of flowers.

Now the little witch stood in the street, very small and lost, and cold in her blue smock and bare feet.

She pointed up at the city clock tower, and it became a huge fir tree, while the clock face turned into a white nodding owl and flew away!

The owl flew as fast as the wind to a tall dark castle perched high on a hill. There at the window sat a slim, tired witch-woman, looking out into the night. "Where, oh where is my little baby witch?"

"Whoo! Whoo!" cried the owl. "There is a little witch down in the city and she is enchanting everything. What will the people say tomorrow?"

The witch-woman rode her broomstick through the sky and over the city, looking eagerly down through the mists.

Far below she could see the little witch running and hiding in doorways, while the kitten chased after her.

Down flew the witch-woman — down, down to a shop doorway. The little witch and the kitten stopped and stared at her.

"Why," said the witch-woman, in her dark velvety voice, "you are my own dear little witch . . . my lost little witch!" She held out her arms and the little witch ran into them. She wasn't lost any more.

The witch-woman looked around at the enchanted city, and she smiled. "I'll leave it as it is," she said, "for a surprise tomorrow."

Then she gathered the little witch onto her broomstick, and the kitten jumped on, too, and off they went to their tall castle home, with windows as deep as night, and lived there happily ever after.

And the next day when the people got up and came out to work, the city was full of flowers and the echoes of laughter.

Junk Day
on Juniper Street

LILIAN MOORE

How did it begin?

No one on Juniper Street can really say.

Benny and Jenny say it began in their house.

Debby says it really began in her backyard.

But Davy thinks his father started it all.

One morning Davy's father was reading his newspaper.

"Take a look at this!" he said to Davy's mother.

DO YOU HAVE JUNK
AROUND YOUR HOUSE?
THEN IT'S
CLEAN-UP TIME!

"Do we have junk?" asked Davy.

"Well . . ." said his mother.

Later, Davy's mother and Debby's mother met in the backyard.

Davy's mother said, "Look at this." And she showed her the newspaper.

"Do we have junk?" asked Debby.

"Hmmmmmm ..." said her mother.

Later, some parents met to have coffee. They met at Benny and Jenny's house.

"Did you see this?" asked Debby's mother. And she showed them the newspaper.

Jenny asked, "Do we have junk?"

All the parents began to laugh.

"We all have junk," they said. "Lots and lots of junk!"

Then someone said, "Let's do it! Let's have a Take-Out-All-the-Junk-Day!"

So Juniper Street had a Junk Day.

It was a big clean-up time in every house.

Mothers and fathers and children walked from one room to the next, saying, "Do we need this any more? Do we want to keep that?"

Then everyone began to put out the junk
- the old chairs
- the old tables
- the old toys and pictures and books.
And every time they looked around the house, people saw more junk to take out
- an old lamp
- a yellow bird cage
- a big rocking chair.
Soon there was a pile of junk outside every house on Juniper Street.

Davy's father looked up and down the street.

"Wow!" he said. "We will need a big truck to take all this away!"

Benny's father called up the junk man.

"We have lots of junk on Juniper Street," he told the man. "You will need a big truck to take it all."

"I have a big truck," said the junk man. "But I can't come today. I will come for your junk in the morning."

"Don't forget," said Benny's father. "A big truck."

All day, people walked past the piles of junk on Juniper Street.

It was hard to go by without taking a good look.

Davy stopped outside Debby's house.

"Say, there's a good wheel!" he cried. "I need a wheel like that for my wagon.

May I have it?"

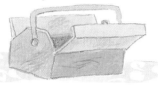

Debby's mother said yes.

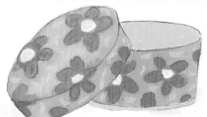

Later Debby's father stopped to look at the junk outside Davy's house. He saw an old tool box.

"Why, it's just what I need!" he said.

"Take it!" said Davy's father.

Soon many people were saying, "Take it!"

Jenny's mother saw a little table she liked.

"I need a little table in the little room," she said.

Debby's mother found a big hatbox in the junk outside Jenny's house. "I can keep my big red hat in this," she said happily.

Jenny saw a doll's bed across the street. She took her doll Amanda across the street and put her in the bed.

"It's just like the three bears," she told Amanda, "not too big, not too little, but just right!"

So Jenny asked for the doll's bed.

By this time everyone was visiting the junk next door and the junk across the street.

A man picked up a lamp.

"Do you call this junk?" he said.
"I can fix this lamp in no time."

And off he went with it.

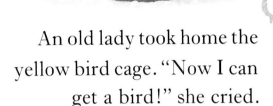

An old lady took home the yellow bird cage. "Now I can get a bird!" she cried.

Someone was happy to find a window box.

"I'll paint it green," he said, "and put in some red geraniums."

Someone saw an old picture of the sea.

"I lived by the sea when I was a boy," he said, and he took the picture home.

By the time the sun went down, there was no more junk on Juniper Street – well, almost none.

One thing was left.

It was a big rocking chair.

Many people stopped to look at it but everyone said, "Too big!"

So there it stood.

The next morning a big truck came down Juniper Street.

"Oh my," said Benny's father. "We forget to tell the junk man not to come!"

The truck came slowly down the street and stopped.

The man who got out of the truck was big, too.

He looked up and down the street.

All he saw was the rocking chair.

He walked over and looked at it.

Then he sat down and began to rock.

"At last!" he said happily. "A big rocking chair!"

Then he put the chair on his truck, and off he went with all the junk on Juniper Street.

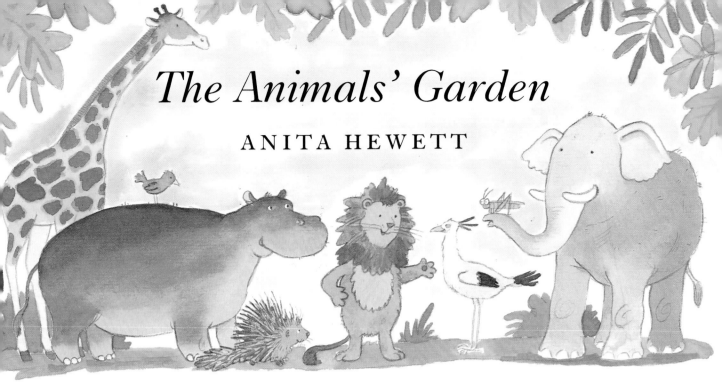

The Animals' Garden

ANITA HEWETT

"A Princess is coming to visit our country," said Lion. "Now how can we show her how happy we are to see her?"

"We could bow very low, and smile," said Hippo. "But some of us aren't the right shape for bowing, and smiling isn't enough by itself."

"We could show the princess how fast we can run," said Giraffe.

"Or jump!" added Grasshopper. "But some of us aren't very good at running or jumping."

"We could cheer," said Porcupine.

"Or trumpet!" added Elephant. "But perhaps the Princess would be frightened."

"We could dance," said Secretary Bird.

Lion looked at Hippo and tried to imagine him dancing. He shook his head, and the animals stared at each other and sighed.

41

Small Brown Bird, who had listened quietly, opened his beak and chirruped shyly: "Couldn't we make a garden, Lion? Princesses love flowers."

Everyone stared at Small Brown Bird.

"That's quite a good idea," said Lion. "We can all help to make a garden."

First, the animals chose a piece of land.

"But it's much too rough," said Lion. "We must break up those big, hard lumps of earth."

"I will do that," cried Hippo at once. "My feet are large and my body is heavy." He stamped on the earth with his big feet, until it was smooth and fine.

"Good!" said Lion. "Now we must make some tiny holes in which to plant the flower seeds."

"I will do that," Porcupine cried. "The spines on my back are very sharp." He curled himself up into a prickly

ball, and rolled over and over the earth until it was covered with tiny holes.

"Good!" said Lion. "Now we must plant seeds."

"I will do that," Grasshopper cried. "I am light and quick."

He jumped lightly and quickly over the earth, planting the seeds.

"Good!" said Lion. "Now we must write the names of the flowers on the wooden labels, so that we know which is which."

"I will do that," cried Secretary Bird. "I have plenty of quills."

He took one of the quills from his head, and wrote the names of the flowers on the labels.

"Good!" said Lion. "Now we must water the garden all over."

"I will do that," Elephant cried. "I will use my trunk." He filled his trunk at the river, and spouted water all over the garden.

"Good!" said Lion. "Now we must keep a look-out for Monkey, so that he won't come and spoil our garden."

"I will do that," cried Giraffe. He stretched his long neck, and peered this way and that, keeping a look out for Monkey.

Small Brown Bird hung his head. He had wanted to help in making the garden. But it seemed that a small brown bird was useless for helping to make a garden.

The tiny seedlings began to grow. But when Lion looked at the garden one day, he shook his head and growled in his throat.

"Those weeds that are growing are ugly," he said. "They will spoil our garden. Now who will pull out all those ugly weeds?"

None of the animals spoke at first. They looked at the ground and shuffled their feet. Then Hippo said in a sulky voice: "I'm sure that I can't pull out the weeds. My feet are too big; they would crush the seedlings."

"My spines would scratch the leaves," said Porcupine.

"The weeds are much too heavy for me," said Grasshopper.

"My stiff feather quills would bruise the buds," said Secretary Bird.

"My trunk would break the stems," said Elephant.

"It's no good looking at me," said Giraffe. "As you very well know, my neck is so long that I can't stoop down."

The lazy animals turned their backs on the weeds.

Small Brown Bird flew down to the garden. With his tiny beak he tugged at a weed, then flew away with the weed in his beak, and dropped it behind a prickly thorn bush. Then back he flew to the garden again to tug at another weed. All through the long, hot, tiring day, Small Brown Bird worked in the garden, pulling the weeds up one by one. The roots were strong and his beak was tiny, so the pile of weeds was still a very little one, when the sun went down behind the hills and Small Brown Bird had to rest. But when he closed his eyes and slept, he dreamed that the Princess smiled at him kindly.

Day after day, Small Brown Bird weeded the garden. There were times when his wings ached with tiredness, and when the weeds hurt his beak.

But one beautiful day, his work was finished. The pile of weeds behind the thorn bush was nearly as high as the thorn bush itself. Small Brown Bird looked at the garden, and not one weed could he see. The red and blue and yellow flowers had grown up straight and tall and lovely.

The very next day, Giraffe looked out over the trees and shouted: "She's coming! I see her! The Princess is coming."

The animals gathered around the garden, but Small Brown Bird flew to a tree, and peeped at the lovely Princess through the leaves.

The Princess smiled when she saw the garden.

"It's the prettiest garden I've ever seen. Did you really make for me?" she said.

"Yes, we made it for you, Princess," said the animals.

"You must have worked very hard indeed."

"Yes, we worked very hard, Princess," said the animals, smiling proudly.

"Will you give me some of your beautiful flowers? Now, who will pick them?" smiled the Princess.

Lion stepped foward. "I told everyone what to do, so I should pick the flowers," he said.

"I broke up the earth," said Hippo.

"I made holes for the seeds," said Porcupine.

"I planted the seeds," said Grasshopper.

"I wrote the labels," said Secretary Bird.

"I watered the garden," said Elephant.

"I kept a look-out for Monkey," said giraffe.

The Princess smiled.

"Tell me," she said. "Who weeded the garden?"

None of the animals answered her question. They looked at the ground and shuffled their feet.

The Princess looked up at the tree in which Small Brown Bird was hiding. She saw two bright eyes and a tiny beak.

"Did you do the weeding, Small Brown Bird?" the Princess asked with a smile.

Small Brown Bird nodded his head.

"Then you shall pick the flowers for me."

Small Brown Bird flew down to the garden. With his tiny beak he picked a flower, and put it into the hands of the lovely Princess. He picked another and another until the Princess held a beautiful bunch of red and blue and yellow flowers.

Then the Princess kissed his small brown head, and smiled at him kindly. Small Brown Bird was very happy. He sang until the sun went down, and he never forgot the lovely Princess.

Big Sister and Little Sister

CHARLOTTE ZOLOTOW

Once there was a big sister and a little sister. The big sister always took care. Even when she was skipping, she took care that her little sister stayed on the path. When she rode her bicycle, she gave her little sister a ride. When she was walking to school, she took the little sister's hand and helped her across the road. When they were playing in the fields, she made sure little sister didn't get lost. When they were sewing, she made sure little sister's needle was threaded and that little sister held the scissors the right way. Big sister took care of everything, and little sister thought there was nothing big sister couldn't do. Little sister would sometimes cry, but big sister always made her stop. First she'd put her arm around her, then she'd hold out her handkerchief and say, "Here, blow."

Big sister knew everything.

"Don't do it like that," she'd say. "Do it this way."

And little sister did. Nothing could bother big sister. She knew too much.

But one day little sister wanted to be alone. She was tired of big sister saying,

"Sit here."

"Go there."

"Do it this way."

"Come along."

And while big sister was getting lemonade and biscuits for them, little sister slipped away, out of the house, out of the garden, down the road and into the meadows where daisies and grass hid her. Very soon she heard big sister calling, calling and calling her. But she didn't answer. She

heard big sister's voice getting louder when she was close and fainter when she went the other way, calling, calling. Little sister leaned back in the daisies. She thought about the lemonade and the biscuits. She thought about the book big sister had promised to read to her. She thought about big sister saying,

"Sit here."

"Go there."

"Do it this way."

"Come along."

No one told little sister anything now. The daisies bent back and forth in the sun. A big bee bumbled by. The weeds scratched her bare legs. But she didn't move. She heard her big sister's voice coming back. It came closer and closer and closer. And suddenly big sister was so near, little sister could have touched her.

Big sister sat down in the daisies. She stopped calling. And she began to cry. She cried and cried just the way little sister often did. When the little sister cried, the big one comforted her. But there was no one to put an arm around big sister. No one took out a handkerchief and said, "Here, blow." Big sister just sat there crying all alone.

Little sister stood up, but big sister didn't even see her, she was crying so much. Little sister went over and put her arm around big sister. She took out her handkerchief and said kindly, "Here, blow."

Big sister did. Then the little sister hugged her.

"Where have you been?" big sister asked.

"Never mind," said little sister. "Let's go home and have some lemonade."

And from that day on little sister and big sister both took care of each other because little sister had learned from big sister and now they both knew how.

The Giant Who Threw Tantrums

DAVID L. HARRISON

At the foot of Thistle Mountain lay a village.

In the village lived a little boy who liked to go walking. One Saturday afternoon he was walking in the woods when he was startled by a terrible noise.

He scrambled quickly behind a bush.

Before long a huge giant came stamping down the path.

He looked upset.

"Tanglebangled ringlepox!" the giant bellowed. He banged his head against a tree until the leaves shook off like snowflakes.

"Franglewhangled whippersnack!" he roared. Yanking up the tree, he whirled it around his head and knocked down twenty-seven other trees.

Muttering to himself, he stalked up the path towards the top of Thistle Mountain.

The little boy hurried home.

"I just saw a giant throwing a tantrum!" he told everyone in the village.

They only smiled.

"There's no such thing as a giant," the Mayor assured him.

"He knocked down twenty-seven trees," said the little boy.

"Must have been a tornado," the weatherman said with a nod. "Happens around here all the time."

The next Saturday afternoon the little boy again went walking. Before long he heard a horrible noise. Quick as lightning, he slipped behind a tree.

Soon the same giant came storming down the path. He still looked upset.

"Pollywogging frizzelsnatch!" he yelled. Throwing himself down, he pounded the ground with both fists.

Boulders bounced like hailstones.

Scowling, the giant puckered his lips into an "O".

He drew in his breath sharply. It sounded like somebody slurping soup.

"Pooh!" he cried.

Grabbing his left foot with both hands, the giant hopped on his right foot up the path towards the top of Thistle Mountain.

The little boy hurried home.

"That giant's at it again," he told everyone. "He threw such a tantrum that the ground trembled!"

"Must have been an earthquake," the police chief said. "Happens around here sometimes."

The next Saturday afternoon the little boy again went walking. Before long he heard a frightening noise.

He dropped down behind a rock.

Soon the giant came fuming down the path. When he reached the little boy's rock, he puckered his lips into an "O". He drew in his breath sharply with a loud, rushing-wind sound. "Phooey!" he cried. "I never get it right!"

The giant held his breath until his face turned blue and his eyes rolled up. "Fozzlehumper backawacket!" he panted. Then he lumbered to the path towards the top of Thistle Mountain.

The little boy followed him. Up and up and up he climbed to the very top of Thistle Mountain.

There he discovered a huge cave. A surprising sound was coming from it. The giant was crying!

"All I want is to whistle," he sighed through his tears. "But every time I try, it comes out wrong!"

The little boy had just learned to whistle. He knew how hard it could be. He stepped inside the cave.

The giant was surprised. "How did you get here?"

"I know what you're doing wrong," the little boy said.

When the giant heard that, he leaned down and put his hands on his knees.

"Tell me at once!" he begged.

"You have to stop throwing tantrums," the little boy told him.

"I promise!" said the giant, who didn't want anyone to think he had poor manners.

"Pucker your lips . . . " the little boy said.

"I always do!" the giant assured him.

"Then blow," the little boy added.

"Blow?"

"Blow."

The giant looked as if he didn't believe it. He puckered

his lips into an "O". He blew. Out came a long, low whistle. It sounded like a railway engine. The giant smiled.

He shouted, "I whistled! Did you hear that? I whistled!"

Taking the little boy's hand, he danced in a circle.

"You're a good friend," the giant said.

"Thank you," said the little boy. "Perhaps some time we can whistle together. But just now I have to go. It's my suppertime."

The giant stood before his cave and waved good-bye.

The little boy seldom saw the giant after that. But the giant kept his promise about not throwing tantrums.

"We never have earthquakes," the Mayor liked to say.

"Haven't had a tornado in ages," the weatherman would add.

Now and then they heard a long, low whistle somewhere in the distance.

"Must be a train," the police chief would say.

But the little boy knew his friend the giant was walking up the path towards the top of Thistle Mountain — whistling.

The Little Girl's Medicine

MARGARET WISE
BROWN

Once upon a time there was a little girl who lived way out in the country on a big tobacco farm. She had no brothers and sisters. She had no one to play with, this poor little girl, and she had to play all by herself. She played all by herself year after year and talked to her parents when they ate their meals.

One day, the little girl became sick. No one knew what was the matter. It was in late August, when they hitched up the four black mules and hauled the tobacco plants away to the big drying barns. But the little girl didn't want to go with them and drive the four big mules. She just sat.

That night there was peach ice cream for dinner, but the little girl didn't want any. She just sat. When it was time to go to bed, she didn't even care.

"Oh dear," said her mother to her father, "our little girl is sick. She loves to drive the four black mules, and yet she wouldn't go with them. She just sat. And she loves peach ice cream, but she wouldn't eat it tonight. She just sat. And she didn't even want to stay up and play when it was time to go to bed. Our little girl must be sick."

So they took the little girl to the doctor in the city.

The little girl's mother said to the doctor in the big city, "Doctor, my little girl is very sick."

"What is the matter with your little girl?" asked the doctor. "Has she a sore throat?"

And the little girl's mother said, "Doctor, my little girl doesn't want to drive the mules any more, and she doesn't like peach ice cream any more, and she doesn't care whether it is bedtime or not. So I fear that she must be a very sick little girl."

"What!" said the doctor, "doesn't like peach ice cream! This is serious! Little girl, stick out your tongue."

So the little girl stuck out her tongue, and the doctor looked at it very carefully. "It is a perfectly good tongue that you have in your head, little girl," said the doctor. "Let me see your throat, little girl. Say Ahhhhhhhh."

So the little girl leaned her head way back, way back, and opened her mouth so wide that she looked like a baby robin asking for food. The doctor took a flashlight and peered down into the little girl's throat. "Say Ahhhhhhhh," he said.

Then he said, "Little girl, let me feel your pulse." So he held the little girl's wrist in his hand, and with his fingers he listened very carefully.

"It's a perfectly good heart that you have in you, little girl; but if you don't like to play any more and don't like peach ice cream any more, you are very sick. It would be a pity if your brothers and sisters caught what is wrong with you."

"But I have no brothers and sisters," said the little girl.

"But your cousins and friends might catch it," said the doctor.

"Only I haven't any cousins; and I haven't any friends," said the little girl.

"Then the small animals on the place might catch it," said the doctor.

"There aren't even any small animals," said the little girl. "Not even a little pig. Just four big old black mules

that kick every time anyone goes near them."

"Well," said the doctor, "this is serious. I will have to prescribe something to make you well."

The doctor sat there for a long time nodding his head. Then at last he said,

"Little girl, I have just the thing that will make you well." So he took out his pencil and wrote it down on a piece of paper, folded it, and handed it to the little girl's mother.

The little girl's mother thanked the doctor, and went out of his office with the little girl.

"We will go right to the drug store first thing," said the little girl's mother, "and have this prescription filled before lunch." So they went into the drug store next door, and the little girl's mother handed the prescription to the druggist, still folded up as the doctor had given it to her.

The druggist was an old man, and he unfolded it slowly.

"Hmmmp," he said. Then he said it again. "Hmmmmp! Do you expect me to fill this prescription?"

"Why, of course," said the little girl's mother. "Haven't you got that kind of medicine?"

Then the druggist, old as he was, just threw back his head and hollered with laughter. "Do you know what this prescription says?" he asked.

The little girl's mother took the prescription and read it. And this is what the prescription said —

PRESCRIPTION

One fat puppy dog
to be given to
the little girl
immediately.
Signed
Dr Wwwww.

"I have filled prescriptions for thirty years," said the druggist, "but never a prescription for a puppy dog. — But wait!" he said. "Wait a minute. — I —think that I can fill this prescription after all. Right across the street. Will you come with me?" he said.

So the little girl and her mother followed the druggist, still chortling and laughing to himself, out of the door and across the street to a house that had a back yard. And there in a box was one furry little puppy dog all by himself.

"This is the last one left," said the druggist. "They belong to my sister, and she is giving them away. So if the doctor says the little girl needs a puppy, this is how we can fill the prescription."

"My puppy?" asked the little girl. "All mine?"

"Yes," said the druggist. "That is your puppy, and you can take him right home with you this minute."

The little puppy wiggled and jumped around the little girl as if he was just as glad as she was that they would have each other to play with. He had been sitting all by himself for two long days. He hadn't even drunk the milk that was still in his saucer.

So the little girl took her puppy right home with her. They got back just as the big wagon with the four black mules was going out of the gate. The little girl's father was driving.

"Hey, little girl," he called, "do you want to go out after the last load with me?"

"Indeed I do!" said the little girl. "And look what I am going to bring with me!"

She jumped out of the car with the puppy under her arm and climbed up on the wagon beside her father.

"For goodness sakes!" he said. "What in the world have you got there?"

"This," said the little girl, "is my medicine, and I feel much better already."

"Well, come here, Medicine," said the little girl's father. "Are you going to learn to be a good tobacco farmer like me and the little girl?"

Little fat Medicine (for that was the puppy's name from then on) wiggled right up in her father's arms and licked him on the nose, and they all drove along on the wagon together behind the four black mules. Then they went home to supper.

And what do you think they had for dessert, and the fat little puppy had a spoonful of it, too? Peach ice cream.

And when it was time to go to bed, up the steps scampered the little girl, and up the steps scampered the little puppy. And together that night the little girl and her Medicine went right off to sleep, all curled up in their warm little beds in the same room.

Big Bakes a Cake

SUE LIMB

Big and Little lived in a house by the sea. Big was so very large that if he came to your house, his head would nearly touch the ceiling. And Little was so small that he lived down the plughole in Big's bath. They were the best of friends, and this was their song:

> My name is Little
> And Big's my name
> If there's ever any trouble
> We're the ones to blame
> We like having picnics
> In the garden and the bath
> And we have a good time
> And dance, sing and laugh.

One day Big and Little had got up late. So they were having their breakfast at lunch time. Big had bought a new breakfast cereal.

"I'm looking forward to this," he said. "It says on the packet it's full of golden goodness and crunchy crackleness and it's made with sugar and honey and all things nice. And when you pour milk on it, it makes the best noise ever."

So Big poured the milk on.
BANG BANG BANG
POPO POOP PPPOOOPPP
WHIZZZ WHIZZZ WHIZZ
BANG BANG BANG

Little ducked down and hid behind an eggcup.

"Good gracious!" he said. "It's deafening! What a racket! It's worse than a cowboy film. My nerves are in shreds! You know how delicate I always feel first thing in the morning! It's terrible!"

Big was munching his way through the first mouthful.

"It tastes terrible, too," he said. "Ugh! Horrible! Much too sweet! It's makin' all my teeth jump!"

"It's all that sugar and honey," said Little. "No wonder it takes me half an hour to walk around you. You ought to eat apples instead, and keep yourself in trim. I'm very very trim."

And he did a few pirouettes on the breadboard to show off how slim he was. But Big wasn't interested.

"Ugh!" he said. "I'll have to have something else — to take away the taste of that horrible cereal."

So Big had bread and jam and ginger nuts and chocolate biscuits and apples and bananas.

"There you are!" he said to Little. "I did have three apples — see?"

"Hasn't the nasty taste gone away yet?" asked Little suspiciously.

"Not quite," said Big. "Nearly, though. I think I'll just have another sixteen marmalade sandwiches. That should do the trick."

But when Big had finished his marmalade sandwiches, the nasty taste had still not gone.

"It's no good," said Big, "I'll have to have some cake. This is an emergency."

"But you've eaten all the cake!" said Little.

"Then I'll just have to go out and buy some."

"But it's Sunday! All the shops are closed."

"Bother!" grumbled Big. "I'll have to make a cake, then." Big hadn't made a cake before, but he didn't tell Little that. He tried to look quite expert and relaxed, and he whistled as he worked.

He got an enormous bowl and put thirty-six eggs in it, and then fifteen pounds of flour and seven pounds of sugar. Then he stirred it with a huge spoon.

"You're making a terrible mess with that cake," said Little, edging backwards. "I don't want nasty sticky goo all over my nice new shoes." So Little climbed up onto a shelf to get out of the way. Big *was* making a mess. The table was already covered with sticky cake mixture and he'd only just started.

"Oh dear," said Big. "What comes next? Eggs, flour, sugar . . . I wish I had a cookbook. I must try and have a think. I hate thinking. It always gives me a pain in the head. Errr . . . no, it's no use. Maybe I should put some tomato sauce in. And a bit of pickle."

"Tomato sauce and pickle! In a cake?" cried Little. "Whatever next? Don't forget the sausages! Hee hee hee!" And Little laughed so hard, he fell off the shelf — right into the cake mixture!

"HELP!" he cried, quite loudly for such a small person. "Help! Nasty, sticky — ugh! Big! Help me! I'm

drowning in horrible muck! Get me out! Help me, Big!"

"Dear, oh dear," said Big with a secret smile. "Poor old Little. Fallen in the cake mix. Here you are then."

And Big pulled him out, and held him up and stared.

"I've never seen such a mess," said Big. "I'll have to put you under the tap to get you clean."

So Big turned the tap on and held Little under it until he was quite clean.

"Help!" shouted Little, struggling as the water ran down his neck. "Help! This water's cold! Stop it, Big! UGH!"

"Dear me!" said Big. "I didn't notice that, Little. I'm sorry. Though they do say cold showers help to keep you in trim. I'll just turn on the other tap."

So Big turned on the hot tap. And he rubbed Little all over with soap.

"Eeeeeeh! Stop it!" giggled Little. "That tickles! And oooooo! Ugh! I've got soapsuds in my mouth!"

And Little spat them out as hard as he could. "All right, all right!" said Little. "Joke's over! Now put me by the fire to dry. And if I get a cold, it'll all be your fault."

"You'll be all right, Little," said Big. "You'll soon be dry. I'll play my whistle and you can dance. Then you'll dry off quicker."

So Big played his whistle, and Little danced, until it was time for tea. By then the cake had cooled, and guess what? It was delicious! So delicious that Big ate four pieces, and Little was really greedy and had three and a half crumbs, and then they both dozed by the fire until it was time for bed.

The Fat Princess

WENDY EYTON

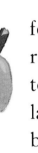

This is a story about a rather fat princess.

She was very pretty and very cuddly, but she found it difficult to squeeze into her dresses when getting ready for balls and banquets — and then she would start to be cross with her lady-in-waiting. It was not the lady-in-waiting's fault that the zips would not zip and buttons would not button, and the princess knew this. But at the banquets and royal feasts, matters went from bad to worse.

The princess, you see, simply could not resist cream cakes, puddings and pastries. Although visiting princes and prime ministers were content with one cream cake, the princess had to have four, or five, and then a helping of jelly and ice cream and a plate of chocolate biscuits.

At one such feast, when the princess was tucking into a large dish of toffee trifle, someone tapped her shoulder

and made her jump in a rather guilty way. She turned to see a frail old lady, with gold-rimmed spectacles, and wings sprouting out of the shoulders of her party dress.

"You won't remember me," said the old lady. "You were a baby when I saw you last — and quite chubby, even then. I am your fairy godmother. I can see that you have a problem and I am going to help you with it."

She muttered some rather nasty-sounding words, touched the princess with a silver wand that had a tarnished star on top, and flew out of the window.

"What does she mean by saying that I have a problem?" muttered the princess. "Just because I'm a bit on the plump side."

There was a sound of tearing material as she reached out for a large meringue — and then a strange thing happened.

The sugary meringue, as soon as she took hold of it, turned into a white and green cauliflower.

The princess looked in amazement at the cauliflower and put it back on the banqueting table. She picked up a brandy-snap and it turned into a large carrot.

"That horrid old woman!" cried the princess. She threw down the carrot, stamped her foot and burst into tears.

Try as she might, the princess could get nothing that she wanted to eat at the banquet. Every time she picked up a cake or a pastry it turned into a vegetable or a piece of fruit. The spell did not only last the evening of the banquet, either. It went on, until the princess became quite slim and sylph-like. But she was not as pretty and cuddly as before, because whenever she saw a stick of rhubarb or a spring onion her face took on a terrible scowl.

But there was one person who did want to help the princess, because he was secretly in love with her, and that was the gardener's boy. The gardener's boy was the seventh son of a seventh son, and very intelligent. And, one day, when he came upon the princess weeping in the royal rose garden, he took off his cap, approached her timidly and said, "Your Highness, I have heard about your royal predicament and think I may have found a way out of it. I understand the problem began with a meringue which turned into a cauliflower. Perhaps you would allow me to escort you to a cauliflower patch I have been tending."

"Cauliflower patch!" cried the princess. "What do I want with a cauliflower patch?"

But she followed the gardener's boy, just the same, because he was already out of earshot and on his way to the royal allotment.

"What you need to do," explained the boy, when the princess caught up with him, "is to reverse your fairy godmother's spell by standing on your head."

The princess opened her mouth to call the guards to throw the gardener's boy into jail for making such a suggestion. But then she saw his blue eyes twinkling at her. And, because she was now so slim, she found standing on her head very easy.

When she was nicely upside down, and had stopped wobbling, the gardener's boy dug up a cauliflower, washed it under the garden hose, and handed it to the princess. As she took it, the cauliflower turned into a big, sugary meringue, with lashings of cream, and chocolate flakes on top. The princess gave a cry of joy and stood on her feet again. But, as soon as she did so, the meringue turned back into a cauliflower.

"You will have to practise eating upside down," said the gardener's boy. "It's easy when you get the hang of it."

And, to make the princess feel better, he stood on his head as well.

The princess was so grateful to the gardener's boy that she asked him to marry her and, as he was the seventh son of a seventh son, he was made a duke immediately and put in charge of the Royal Garden Mint.

At the wedding feast there were long tables laid for guests, crammed with cakes, sweets and pastries and one for the princess laden with vegetables and fruit.

Sometimes the princess stayed the right way up and nibbled at a grapefruit or a piece of celery and sometimes she stood on her head and the celery became icing sugar and the grapefruit a pudding with treacle on top.

But, because of all the exercise involved, she was just the same shape at the end of the banquet as at the beginning of it, and went off for her honeymoon in a hot air balloon.

I think I saw it the other day. It had a large tomato painted on one side and a cream bun on the other.

The princess and the gardener's boy were standing in a basket, waving their arms about. They looked happy as can be.

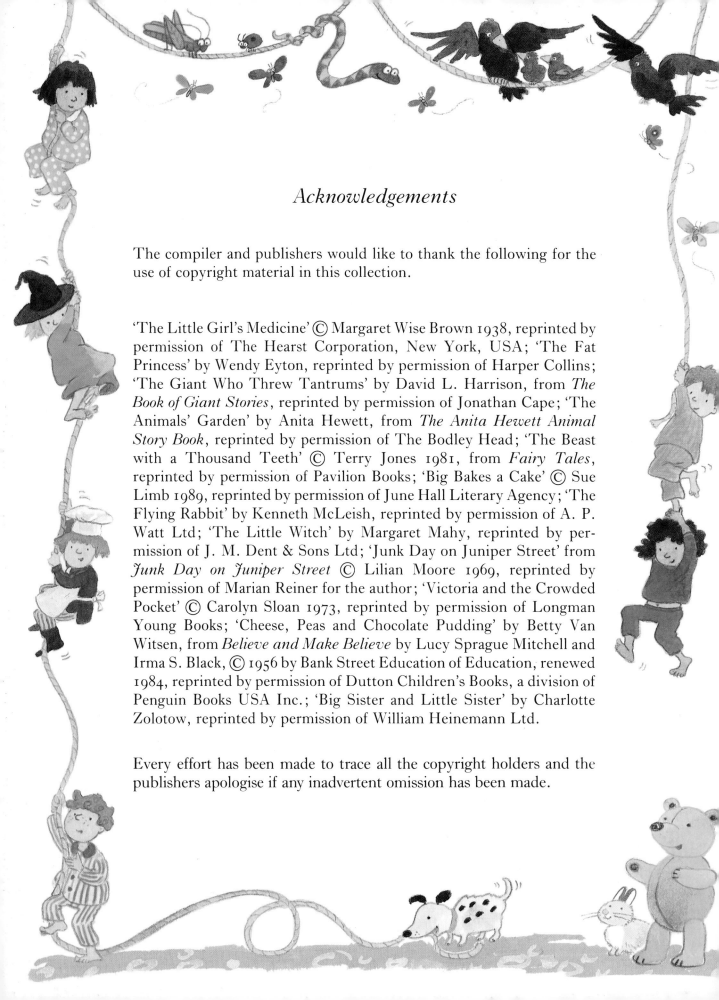

Acknowledgements

The compiler and publishers would like to thank the following for the use of copyright material in this collection.

'The Little Girl's Medicine' © Margaret Wise Brown 1938, reprinted by permission of The Hearst Corporation, New York, USA; 'The Fat Princess' by Wendy Eyton, reprinted by permission of Harper Collins; 'The Giant Who Threw Tantrums' by David L. Harrison, from *The Book of Giant Stories*, reprinted by permission of Jonathan Cape; 'The Animals' Garden' by Anita Hewett, from *The Anita Hewett Animal Story Book*, reprinted by permission of The Bodley Head; 'The Beast with a Thousand Teeth' © Terry Jones 1981, from *Fairy Tales*, reprinted by permission of Pavilion Books; 'Big Bakes a Cake' © Sue Limb 1989, reprinted by permission of June Hall Literary Agency; 'The Flying Rabbit' by Kenneth McLeish, reprinted by permission of A. P. Watt Ltd; 'The Little Witch' by Margaret Mahy, reprinted by permission of J. M. Dent & Sons Ltd; 'Junk Day on Juniper Street' from *Junk Day on Juniper Street* © Lilian Moore 1969, reprinted by permission of Marian Reiner for the author; 'Victoria and the Crowded Pocket' © Carolyn Sloan 1973, reprinted by permission of Longman Young Books; 'Cheese, Peas and Chocolate Pudding' by Betty Van Witsen, from *Believe and Make Believe* by Lucy Sprague Mitchell and Irma S. Black, © 1956 by Bank Street Education of Education, renewed 1984, reprinted by permission of Dutton Children's Books, a division of Penguin Books USA Inc.; 'Big Sister and Little Sister' by Charlotte Zolotow, reprinted by permission of William Heinemann Ltd.

Every effort has been made to trace all the copyright holders and the publishers apologise if any inadvertent omission has been made.